DAVY'S DREAM

Written and Illustrated

by

PAUL OWEN LEWIS

TRICYCLE PRESS
Berkeley, California

TRICYCLE PRESS
P.O. Box 7123
Berkeley, California 94707

Library of Congress Catalog Card Number: 88-070816

First published in 1988 by Beyond Words Publishing
First Tricycle Press printing, 1999
ISBN 1-58246-001-9 Paperback
ISBN 1-58246-000-0 Hardcover

Printed in China

4 5 6 7 8 — 09 08 07 06 05

Other Tricycle Press books by Paul Owen Lewis:
  Grasper
  Storm Boy
  Frog Girl
  P. Bear's New Year's Party

Dedicated to the memory of my friend and father,
GARY BARTON LEWIS.
With thanks to Jasper,
Mimi, and C.B. Johnston.

One sunny afternoon,
a boy named Davy
lay in the tall grass
on a hilltop dreaming.

It was a dream of killer whales.

He saw himself sailing among them

in play,

in song,

in silence,

and in joy.

When he awoke,
he ran down the hill into the harbor town
eager to share his dream of the happy whales
with the people there.

"Ha, wild Orca? They're dangerous," laughed an old fisherman.

"Not like those tame ones doin' tricks."

"Yep, 'Wolves of the Sea' we call 'em around here," agreed another.

"Hunt in packs and eat anything," said yet another, squinting his eyes as he spoke.

Davy suddenly felt very foolish. He told no one else about his dream that day.

But the wonder he felt for the whales
and the memory of the dream
would not leave him.
He sailed out of the harbor
and into the straits
to look for them.

Not long afterwards,
far away on the water's surface,
he saw what looked like little black triangles.

Killer whale fins!

Quickly he trimmed the sails
and raced towards them.
Davy's hopes rose together with the
spray off the bow of the boat.
But, he could soon tell, the whales were
swimming away from him faster than
he could follow.

Once more he trimmed the sails.
Davy's hopes rose
as he raced towards them.
But at the last moment,
the whales dived — and vanished.

He tried again and again,
but always it seemed the whales
would have nothing to do
with the boy in the boat.
"I guess the dream
was just a dream after all,"
Davy said to himself.
He sailed for home.

The next day,
Davy was bored and restless.
With nothing better to do
he climbed back up
his sunny hilltop to think.
As he sat,
the heat of the sun made him drowsy.
He lay down in the grass,
closed his eyes,
fell asleep,
and began
to dream again . . .

When he awoke,
he ran down into the town —
and telling no one . . .

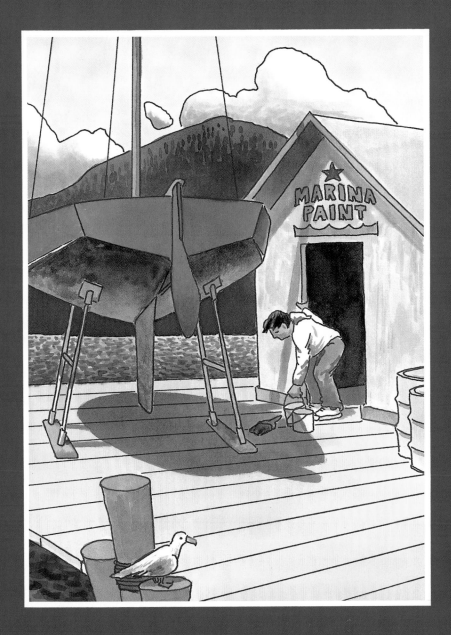

Playing, singing, resting,
and jumping for joy together —
Davy and his new friends had done it all!
But now, the setting sun reminded him that it
would soon be dark. It was time to go home.
Davy waved goodbye,
and the whales each spouted in reply.

The evening air darkened quickly as the little
sailboat glided home alone. Then, without
warning, there was a loud

CRUNCH

and the boat lurched to a stop.
Davy knew at once he must have hit a rock
as water began to fill the boat.
The boat was sinking.

No sooner had he started bailing
when two towering black fins
rose out of the water
on either side of the boat.
The boat began to rise —
and move forward very fast.

In no time at all
Davy was safely back in the harbor.

The next morning, Davy told everything to the fishermen.

"Boy," said the first, "you've been watching too much TV!"

"Imagine that," said the second, "being rescued by wild killer whales. That lad can sure tell a good fish story!"

"Got a screw loose more likely," said the third, squinting his eyes as he spoke.

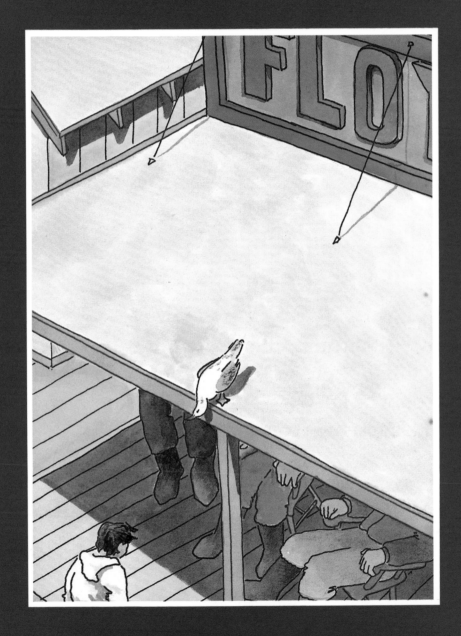

Davy left the men again.
But this time, a great big smile grew on his face.
Because he knew — and you and I know too —
that dreams can come true.